Freddie the Spider

Ruth Emanuel

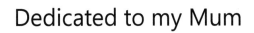

Dedicated to my Mum

Freddie the spider lived with his mummy and daddy in an upside down flower pot at the bottom of Mr & Mrs Brown's garden. It had been left there for many years and was hidden by overgrown ivy so was a safe home for Freddie and his mummy and daddy.

Freddie and his mummy and daddy had made themselves a cosy home inside the flower pot. It had a hole at the top and they were able to climb up to the hole to get in and out of their home. The hole also meant that they could see and hear everything that went on in the garden. Of course, they had to be careful not to be seen by the birds who would want to eat them.

One day Freddie asked his mummy if he could go out of the flower pot and explore. "Yes you can Freddie" said his mummy "but be very careful you don't get seen and caught and make sure you get home before it gets dark". So off Freddie went up the top of the flower pot, out through the hole and into the garden.

Now, Mr & Mrs Brown had two children; they were called Jacob and Gabriella and were five years old. As it was such a warm summer day, Jacob and Gabriella were enjoying themselves playing in the garden.

Gabriella was riding her tricycle and Jacob was playing with his ball. Freddie stood and watched them playing, he loved being outside in the fresh air and sunshine. He saw Mrs Brown come out to the garden with a tray of drinks and biscuits and sat on the grass with the children having a picnic. Freddie was really enjoying his time in the garden in the sunshine.

Mr & Mrs Brown had three large brown chickens that lived in a chicken house also at the bottom of the garden not very far from Freddie's flower pot. The chicken house had a little garden in the front of it, this is called a chicken run, and it was surrounded by a fence to make sure the chickens were safe from a fox getting into their home. Every morning Mr Brown came down the garden to let the chickens into the run and would feed them corn for breakfast.

This particular morning, as the air was so warm Mr Brown decided to let the chickens out into the garden so that they could have a run around and a good peck at the grass. So whilst Freddie was busy watching Jacob and Gabriella playing he didn't notice the chickens running around behind him. He thought he heard a scratching noise and when he turned around he got such a fright! There was a chicken standing right next to him! In fact the chickens foot was about to squash him.

Freddie ran as fast as he could, not looking where he was going; he just wanted to get away from the chickens. He ran and ran until he was quite out of breath and when he stopped he wasn't sure where he was. Once he had stopped huffing and puffing and could breathe again, Freddie looked around to see where he was. He realised that he had run all the way up the garden to where Mrs Brown and the children were having a picnic and that he was standing in the middle of a saucer. Oh no! He had to get away before Mrs Brown saw him but as he went to run off Mrs Brown finished drinking her tea and was about to put her tea cup back on the saucer. Freddie looked up and saw the bottom of the tea cup coming down towards him and with all his strength he ran as fast as he could up the side of the saucer and jumped into the grass, just as Mrs Brown put her cup onto the saucer. Freddie hid in the grass panting and shaking, he was very lucky to have escaped being squashed by the cup and it took him a few minutes to calm down and walk again.

Mrs Brown and the children had finished their picnic and Freddie could see some cake and biscuit crumbs in the grass. He had eaten his breakfast a long time ago and he was really hungry so he waited until Mrs Brown took the picnic tray into the house and the children were busy playing again, and he crept along the grass to the crumbs and nibbled them. They were delicious and he ate all of them until he didn't feel hungry anymore.

The sun was still shining and Freddie didn't want to go home yet, he was having fun and wanted to carry on exploring in the garden for a bit longer. He decided he was going to walk up to the top of the garden and see what it was like so off he went.

Now, Freddie didn't know that Mr & Mrs Brown had a rather large dog. She was a brown Alsatian called Rosie and she lived in a kennel outside at the top of the garden. Just like Freddie, Rosie loved the sunshine and she was lying in the grass fast asleep enjoying the warm air.

Freddie was having a lovely walk in the grass, feeling very pleased with himself when suddenly he heard a rumbling sound and felt hot air blowing on his body. He immediately stopped walking and stood very still wondering what was happening. Another blast of hot air blew at him nearly knocking him over and when he turned around he realised, with horror, that he was standing right in front of a large black wet nose which was blowing out hot air all over him. He knew that the wet nose belonged to the dog that lived in the kennel at the top of Mr & Mrs Brown's house and he became very frightened. How was he going to get away without waking up the dog?

Freddie curled himself into a tight ball hoping that the dog wouldn't see him and he lay very still in the grass, thinking of a plan to escape. He was getting very worried because the sunshine had almost gone and it was nearly the end of the day. Freddie knew that his mummy and daddy would be worried about him. His mummy had told him to get home before it was dark. But then something happened which meant that Freddie could get away. Mr Brown was calling Rosie; he wanted to take her for a walk. After he had called her a couple of times Rosie opened her eyes, jumped up, barked and went running off to the house where Mr Brown was waiting for her. Thank goodness! It was safe for Freddie to go home to his flower pot.

So Freddie uncurled himself, had a quick stretch and ran as fast as he could down to the bottom of the garden, up the side of the flower pot, through the hole and into his cosy home where his mummy and daddy were waiting for him.

"Oh thank goodness you are home Freddie" cried his mummy, "daddy and I have been so worried about you".

Freddie ran up to his mummy and hugged her. "Sorry for being so late mummy, I've had some very big adventures today".

"Well, let's sit down and have supper now and you can tell us all about your day" said daddy.

Freddie did tell his mummy and daddy all about his adventures in the garden and when he went to sleep that night, he dreamt of his lovely day in Mr & Mrs Brown's garden. He couldn't wait for his next visit to the top of the garden.